# Mice Twice

*story & pictures by* $\mathcal{J}OSEPH\ LOW$

*Aladdin Paperbacks*

# For a Particular Mouse

First Aladdin Paperbacks edition 1986

Copyright © 1980 by Joseph Low

Aladdin Paperbacks
An imprint of Simon & Schuster Children's Publishing Division
1230 Avenue of the Americas
New York, NY 10020

Printed in Hong Kong
10   9   8

Library of Congress Cataloging-in-Publication Data
Low, Joseph, 1911–
   Mice twice.
   Summary: A round of uneasy hospitality results when Mouse and
Dog arrive at Cat's house for dinner.
   [1. Animals—Fiction.   2. Etiquette—Fiction]
I. Title.
PZ7.L9598Mi      1986      [E]      85-26768
ISBN 0-689-71060-7 (pbk.)

CAT was thinking about supper.
He thought, "I could eat forty-seven grasshoppers.
Or I could eat sixty-nine crickets.
Or I could eat a fine, fat sparrow.
But what I think I'd *really* like
is a nice, tender mouse."

So he went and sat outside Mouse's door.
"Are you there, Mouse," he asked, "and
in good health, I hope?"

Mouse lay snug in her nest behind the door.
The door was too small for Cat to get through.


"Never better," she said.

Cat tuned his rough voice to make it smooth.
He said, "Such a lovely day! I was just thinking,
'How nice to have a friend for supper.'
I do hope you can join me this evening."

Mouse knew Cat well, and all his cunning ways.
"May I bring a friend?" she asked.

("Mice twice!" thought Cat, licking his whiskers.)
"By all means," he said. "Shall we say six o'clock?"

"Six will be fine," said Mouse.

At six that evening she knocked on Cat's door.
Cat's stomach rumbled. "Come in, come in!" he said.
But when he opened the door, he saw that
Mouse's friend was not another mouse.

It was Dog. Dog was grinning.
He was twice as big as Cat.

Cat was angry, but he was afraid to show it.
He waved them into the house.
On the table were two small bits of cheese.

"Such a warm day!" said Cat. "I find it best not to eat on warm days. But do help yourselves."

So Mouse took one piece of cheese.
And Dog took the other.

When he had swallowed his, Dog said, "I have seldom enjoyed a cheese so much. Is it Swiss?"

"Or is it French?" asked Mouse.

"French," said Cat. "A gift from my cousin Pierre."

(Actually, it was common old rat-trap cheese, as Dog and Mouse knew very well.)

Dog said, "It has been so pleasant, dear Cat.
I hope you will have dinner with me tomorrow night."
Cat thought for a moment. "I will, indeed," he
said, "if I may bring a friend."
"Good company makes for good eating," said Dog.
"Bring any friend you like. Shall we say
seven o'clock?"
"Seven will be fine," said Cat.

At seven the next night, Cat knocked on Dog's
door. Beside him stood Wolf – twice as big
as Dog. Four times as fierce.
"Come in, come in!" called Dog.

Cat looked at Wolf. He whispered, "Dog for you.
Mouse for me. Agreed?"
Wolf said nothing, but curled his lip in a
horrid smile. All his sharp teeth were showing.
Cat and Wolf both licked their whiskers.

But when the door opened,
there beside Dog sat Crocodile.
His big, toothy jaws slowly opened and closed
as he smiled at Cat and Wolf.

Cat and Wolf stared at that gaping mouth. So big!
So red! So many, many teeth! They could not
take their eyes away. Not even to look at
the four pieces of cheese on the table.

"Ummmm," said Wolf,
looking over his shoulder
at the door.

"Actually," said Cat, "we came to ask if we might
make it another night. Neither of us is feeling well."
"What a pity!" said Dog. "I had so hoped you
might enjoy this delicate French cheese.
Brie, it is called."

(And it really *was* French Brie.)

"Another time," mumbled Cat as he and Wolf
backed out the door.

Cat thought for a moment, looking back at
Crocodile. "Tomorrow night," he said, "I'd like you
to meet a distant relative who will be visiting me
for dinner. Can you join me – and bring your friend?"

"Delighted," said Dog.

"But not Crocky, here.
He must get back to the river tonight. Perhaps
Mouse might come, if that is agreeable?"

"Splendid!" said Cat, trying not to grin. "I will
expect you at eight o'clock."

At eight the next evening Dog and Mouse
knocked on Cat's door.
Inside sat Lion, so big he all but filled the
house. Cat had to sit between his huge paws.
Cat was smiling.
In the space remaining at one side was a table.
It was covered with dishes of good things Cat had
bought to please Lion. There were fresh-roasted
peanuts; fat, juicy raisins; little cakes covered
with sugar frosting; bits of fried and crumbled
bacon; and a silver tray of mint candies.

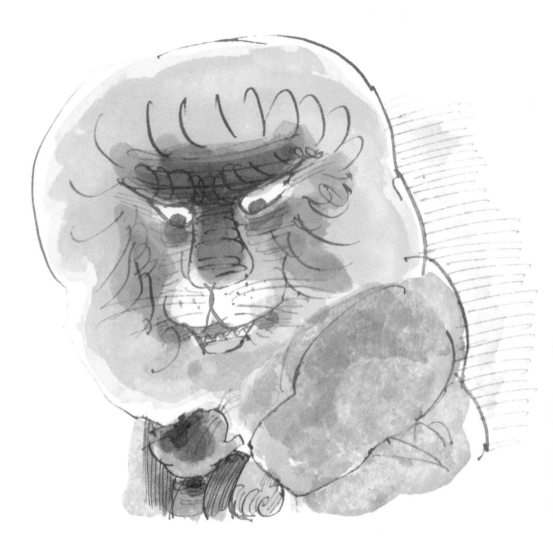

Cat looked up and whispered to Lion,
"When the door opens, I will grab Mouse,
you grab Dog, and that will be that!"
"That!" rumbled Lion, licking his whiskers
with his rough, red tongue.

"How prompt you are!
Come in! Come in!"
cried Cat to Dog.


As the door swung open,
both Cat and Lion leaned forward,
their mouths already open.

Neither of them had noticed that Dog and Mouse
had brought their good friend, Wasp.

Quick as a wink, Wasp stung Lion's nose.
Then his ear. Then his rough, red tongue.
Lion was frantic!

He tried to back away, but Cat's house was
too tight around him.

Wasp stung his lip.

Lion broke the house apart and ran.

Cat ran after him.

And Dog after Cat.

Cat's house was wrecked, but the table was unharmed.

All the good things on it
stood as they had been.

"Good friend," said Mouse to Wasp, "do help yourself
to anything you fancy. Those little cakes, perhaps?
Or one of the mints? I rather like the smell of
those peanuts, myself, for starters. Plenty here
for both of us, and a good share, too, for Dog,
if Cat escapes what he deserves."

If Cat *did* escape, you may be sure he never
bothered Mouse again.